Dear Parent:
Your child's love of reading starts here!

Every child learns to read in a different way and at his or her own speed. Some go back and forth between reading levels and read favorite books again and again. Others read through each level in order. You can help your young reader improve and become more confident by encouraging his or her own interests and abilities. From books your child reads with you to the first books he or she reads alone, there are I Can Read Books for every stage of reading:

SHARED READING
Basic language, word repetition, and whimsical illustrations, ideal for sharing with your emergent reader

BEGINNING READING
Short sentences, familiar words, and simple concepts for children eager to read on their own

READING WITH HELP
Engaging stories, longer sentences, and language play for developing readers

READING ALONE
Complex plots, challenging vocabulary, and high-interest topics for the independent reader

ADVANCED READING
Short paragraphs, chapters, and exciting themes for the perfect bridge to chapter books

I Can Read Books have introduced children to the joy of reading since 1957. Featuring award-winning authors and illustrators and a fabulous cast of beloved characters, I Can Read Books set the standard for beginning readers.

A lifetime of discovery begins with the magical words **"I Can Read!"**

Visit www.icanread.com for information
on enriching your child's reading experience.

HarperCollins®, 🔖®, and I Can Read Book® are trademarks of HarperCollins Publishers.

Iron Man: I Am Iron Man!
Printed in the United States of America. No part of this book may be used or reproduced in any manner
whatsoever without written permission except in the case of brief quotations embodied in critical articles and
reviews. For information address HarperCollins Children's Books, a division of HarperCollins Publishers,
1350 Avenue of the Americas, New York, NY 10019.
www.icanread.com

Library of Congress catalog card number: 2007942254
ISBN 978-0-06-082193-7
❖
First Edition

4143 5602
10/09

I Can Read!™

READING 2 WITH HELP

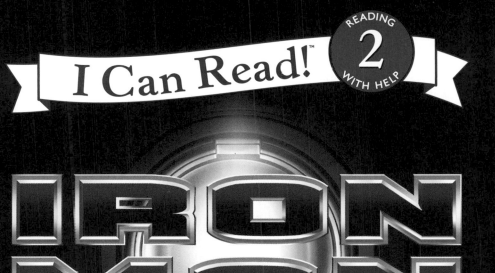

I AM IRON MAN!

Adapted by Lisa Rao

Pictures by Guido Guidi

Based on the motion picture by

Mark Fergus & Hawk Ostby

and Art Marcum & Matt Holloway

HarperCollins*Pub*

Hi, there. My name is Tony Stark.

Maybe you recognize me.

My picture is in the newspapers a lot.

My father was Howard Stark.

He started his own company.

It was called Stark Industries.

My dad built airplanes.

He became a rich and powerful man.

My father died when I was

twenty-one years old.

He left his company to me.

And his fortune!

9

Now I am rich.

I can do whatever I want.

I could keep building airplanes,

but I had another idea.

I wanted to build something

really special!

I started from the bottom up.

The boots I created

looked uncomfortable . . .

. . . and they *were* uncomfortable, at first.

But these boots weren't made for walking.

They were made for flying!

I started off nice and easy.

But I didn't get very far.
I soon learned I had
much more work to do.

I had a few more test flights
in the workshop.
Every day, my creation
became a little bit better.

I was almost ready
to try out my invention
in the real world!

People had not seen me in a while.

So I went on television.

I told everyone

I was working on

a new invention.

STARK INDUSTRIES

My assistant, Pepper,
was by my side.
She was worried
that my invention
was too dangerous.

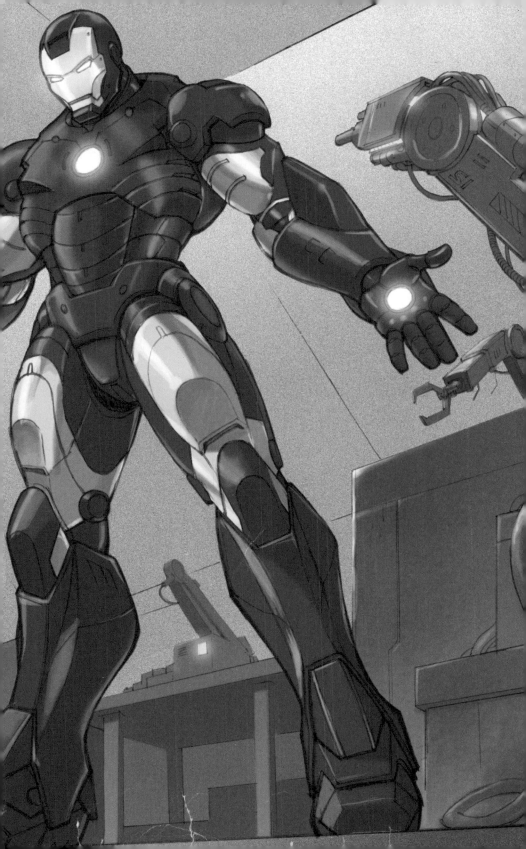

Pepper didn't like the idea.

She wanted me to run more tests.

I didn't want to wait another second!

I said good-bye and took off.

Flying was even better

than I thought it would be!

Who needs an airplane

when you have your own jet power?

I felt like I could
touch the moon!

I waved to a boy on a Ferris wheel.

He couldn't believe his eyes.

I passed a burning building!

I saw a little girl crying in the window.

I knew I could get to her

before the firemen.

I saved her!

I had just enough power left

to get home safely,

so I couldn't stop to talk to anybody.

A lot of people saw me in the sky
while I was out on my test run.

People were asking questions.

But the world would have to wait

to learn my secret!